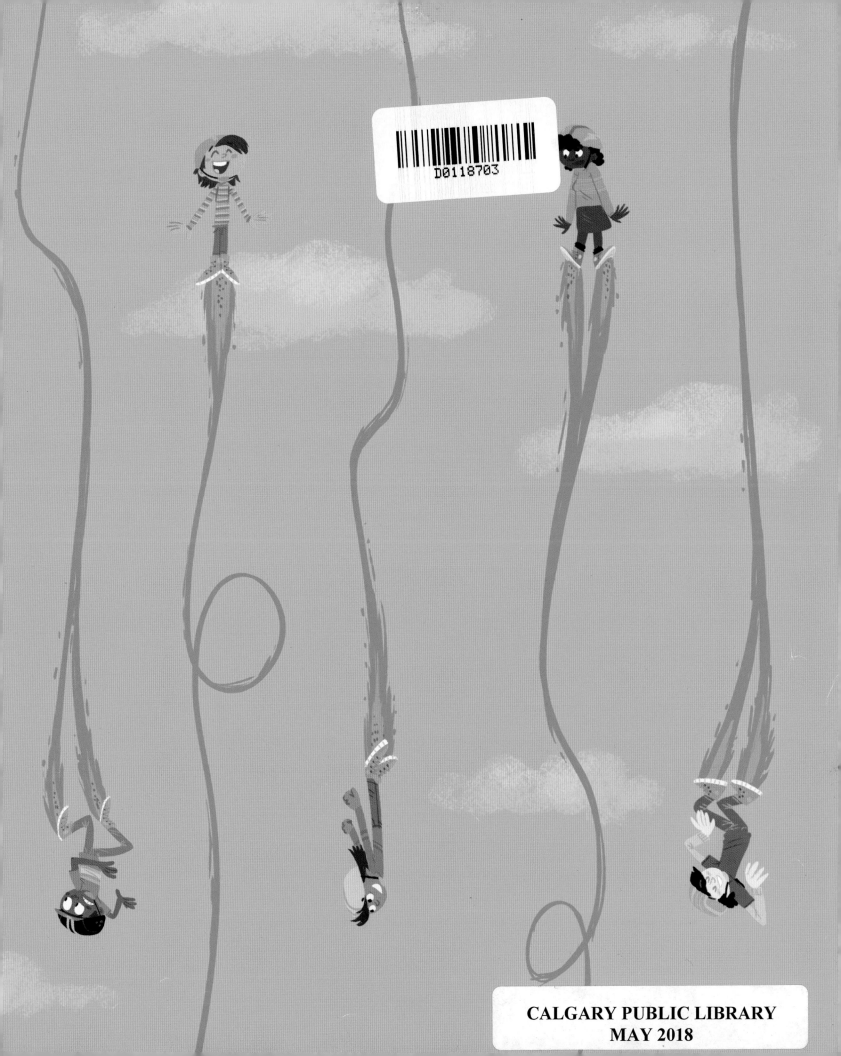

For Zerina:
Dream big, soar high!
(Shoes are optional.)
—S. S.

To Andrea, Ava, and Ezra:
For lifting me up and keeping
me grounded.
—W. J.

STERLING CHILDREN'S BOOKS
New York

An Imprint of Sterling Publishing Co., Inc.
1166 Avenue of the Americas
New York, NY 10036

Text © 2017 Sharon Skinner
Illustrations © 2017 Ward Jenkins

ISBN 978-1-4549-2152-3

Distributed in Canada by Sterling Publishing Co., Inc.
c/o Canadian Manda Group, 664 Annette Street
Toronto, Ontario, Canada M6S 2C8
Distributed in the United Kingdom by GMC Distribution Services
Castle Place, 166 High Street, Lewes, East Sussex, England BN7 1XU
Distributed in Australia by NewSouth Books
45 Beach Street, Coogee, NSW 2034, Australia

For information about custom editions, special sales, and premium and
corporate purchases, please contact Sterling Special Sales at 800-805-5489 or
specialsales@sterlingpublishing.com.

Manufactured in China

Lot #:
2 4 6 8 10 9 7 5 3 1
07/17

sterlingpublishing.com

The artwork for this book was created with digital media.
Design by Ryan Thomann

Rocket Shoes

by
Sharon Skinner

illustrated by
Ward Jenkins

STERLING CHILDREN'S BOOKS
New York

"**Shoes** with engines, springs, and sprockets, kick-start heels, and shoe-size rockets."

"Shoes with jets and jazzy laces,
flying kids to far-off places."

In his dreams, when all is quiet,
José is a jet shoe pilot.

Ma says, "*Hijo*, I'm not buying crazy kids' shoes just for flying."

So, José works and
scrapes and saves,

selling cups of lemonade,

scrubbing cars

and mowing lawns,

walking dogs from dusk 'til dawn.

He earns enough to buy a pair—
"Guaranteed to glide on air."

He straps them on and, with a cheer,
jets into the atmosphere.

Zooming, zipping, hopping, soaring.
Sky-high flying, world-exploring.

Flipping, spinning, ninja kicks.
Bold and daring airborne tricks.

But Mrs. Greg begins to nag,
when overhead, some kids play tag.

"They wreck our trees."

"They scare the squirrels!"

"We're ducking boys and dodging girls!"

Adults protest with signs held high.
"Kids were never meant to fly!"

The mayor says, "I'm not amused.
I hereby ban all rocket shoes."

José stares at the empty sky
and dreams of when he used to fly.

No zooming, zipping, hopping, soaring.
No more sky-high, world exploring.

No flipping, spinning, ninja kicks.
No more daring airborne tricks.

A storm arrives. A giant freeze!
It dumps out snow and knocks down trees.

In José's room, he hears a yelp,
a desperate noise, a cry for help!

It's Mrs. Greg! She waves and shouts,
"My cat is gone. He wandered out!"

She tries to cross the snowy sweep
but sinks into a drift nose-deep.

Snow piles up and, in a snap,
it covers up her knitted cap.

José searches every box,
on shelves, in drawers, behind his socks.

Beneath his bed, he finds them hidden,
but rocket shoes are still forbidden.

Should he?
Yes? Or maybe no?
But Mrs. Greg is
under snow!

He slips them on, ties them tight,
and blasts off in a frantic flight.

He flies into the blinding snow
and finds a frozen hand below.

He grabs on tight, then pulls and lifts,
to save her from the freezing drifts.

He flies her home and while she thaws,

he saves her cat and warms its paws.

When word gets out, the mayor calls
a public meeting at Town Hall.

She greets José and pats his back,

then hands him an enormous plaque.

She says, "Jose, I heard the news.
You broke the rules and wore those shoes."

"But just this once, I'll let it slide.
We're glad you gave that airlift ride."

"I'll lift the ban, but I insist,
rooftop tag is off the list!"

"Instead we'll build a special place
where kids can jet and whiz and race."

Kids and parents, side-by-side,
dip and soar and dive and glide.

They speed through clouds,
make swoops and arcs at José Felix Flying Park.

Zooming, zipping, hopping, soaring.
Sky-high flying, world-exploring.

Flipping, spinning, ninja kicks.

Mrs. Greg does airborne tricks.